The Autobiography of The Taj

Editor
Vandita Sharma

ISO 9001:2008 GVE
GYAN VIGYAN EDUCARE

Published by
Gyan Vigyan Educare
3639 Netaji Subhash Marg, Darya Ganj,
New Delhi-110 002

ISBN 978-93-84344-35-1
THE AUTOBIOGRAPHY OF THE TAJ
Ed. Vandita Sharma

Edition
First, 2015

Price
₹ 150.00 (Rupees One Hundred Fifty only)

Printed at
R-Tech Offset Printers, Delhi

For all my students and
my children Anumeha and Varun

"The future belongs to those who believe in the beauty of their dreams."

—Eleanor Roosevelt

Contents

Acknowledgement

Every great experience requires the efforts of many to be truly good. When this project was being made I had never thought that one day it would be published as a book and be read by many.

I would like to take this opportunity to thank all those who made this journey an enriching and a memorable experience. There are many people who have been a part of this journey.

I am grateful to my school Birla Balika Vidyapeeth and my Principal Dr. M. Kasturi for giving me the opportunity for working on the project 'Seven Wonders of the World'. At that time I had no clue that the project would turn out so well.

I would like to thank all my students who were pivotal in making this dream project come true. This project brought a sense of pride, satisfaction and accomplishment to all of my students who joined hands to make this effort. They proved that they just need a platform to showcase their creativity and ability.

Asawari Keskar was the one who initiated the project by writing the Autobiography. Meghna Jain, helped in the Cover Design. I explained to them what I wanted and they transformed my thoughts into words and design.

Isha Nagpal, Garima Sharma and Anampreet wrote about their visit to the Taj and their experience, which is in the form of a skit.

The introductions for the Seven Wonders were given by Jasmine Kumar, Gayatri Vyas, Saras Agarwal, Ananya Varshney, Samidha Bharati, Parisha Gupta, Sonam Verma and Khushi Saini.

The poems are the works of my students who showed their creativity by writing beautiful poems. The students are different yet they joined in to form a complete whole. This Project was a journey of experience, which would not have been completed, had it not been for them.

I would also like to thank Ms. Anita Mishra (Senior Coordinator), Ms. Sita Kumar (HOD, English) for their inspiring words, A special word for Ms. Seema Sinha who helped me in editing My special thanks to Prof. Pushplata (Dept. of English, BITS Pilani) for her words of wisdom and guidance. Not to forget, all my friends for their motivation and unconditional support in this memorable journey.

I am highly indebted to Garima's Dadaji Shri Shanta Kumar, who helped me find a publisher to get this book published. He not only encouraged and inspired me, but also helped in getting the works of my students published. He is the one who made my dream of getting this book published a reality. My sincere thanks to him.

Last but not the least, my pillars of support, my children, Anumeha and Varun, for being an inspiration and unstinting supports in all my ventures. Love you both. You both are my world.

Introduction

'A Thing of Beauty is a Joy Forever, Its loveliness increases...' John Keats

With this note, I begin the Introduction of *The Autobiography of the Taj*. The project began when we went on a Grand tour of the Taj Mahal. I had nothing in my mind. It seemed as if my mind had gone blank. But thinking about Taj, reminded me of its grandeur, the story behind this beautiful apostle of love, and the thought of writing the *Autobiography* came to my mind.

Before initiating this project, I discussed this theme with my students. My students loved it and thus was born *'The Autobiography of The Taj'*.

My students researched on all the Seven Wonders of the World and they came to the conclusion that the world submits before their beauty. What makes these wonderful pieces of art all the more significant and worthwhile is the fact that they are backed by a history rich in art, culture and heritage.

It is in the nature of human race to strive for perfection and the various creations of mankind are proof of this insatiable human desire to reach for the summit of the ideal and aspire for the heights of glory. Since time immemorial, man has attempted to give expression to the artistic aspect of his mind through the creation of awe-inspiring architectures that are still a source of amazement and wonder for the modern generation.

The quest for perfection made them reach out in giving expression to their thoughts and imagination. The result is a rich tapestry of all the wonders of the world. They proved that '*Beauty lies in the Eyes of the Beholder....*'

This project is a joint venture of my students of Class IX-A, X-B, X-D who transformed my ideas and thoughts to make this dream project a reality. It was a mammoth task selecting, compiling and editing this project but I enjoyed this journey.

I hope, just as it was for me, this project proves to be a memorable journey of visiting the Wonders of the World, through the eyes of the Taj.

—Vandita Sharma

Dept. of English

Birla Balika Vidyapeeth

Pilani (Rajasthan)

The Autobiography of The Taj

Taj's Introduction to The Seven Wonders

I am Taj – The Taj Mahal, the pride of India. I was recently voted the first, out of the seven wonders of the world, namely Me (the Taj Mahal in Agra, India), The Chichen Itza (Mexico), The Great Wall of China (China), The Statue of Christ the Redeemer (Brazil), The Colosseum (Italy), The Petra (Jordan) and The Machu Picchu (Peru). I feel proud to be adored by the people all over the globe and am self-satisfied when by being a crucial fascination for the tourists, I contribute significantly to the Indian economy. I am proud to be known as an eternal symbol of love.

But, before I narrate my story, I would like to tell you about the other six wonders that stand tall in the world along with me.

The Chichen Itza (Mexico)
The Great Wall of China (China)
The Statue of Christ the Redeemer (Brazil)
The Colosseum (Italy)
The Petra (Jordan)
The Machu Picchu (Peru)

7
NEW
WONDERS
OF THE WORLD
$1.40

'All things bright and beautiful,
All things great and small,
All things wide and wonderful,
Good God made them all.'

God is the Creator of everything around us. He also created humans who have embellished this world with monuments. Some of these are known as 'THE SEVEN WONDERS OF THE WORLD.'

Everlasting Wonders

Since the archaic times, under the azure sky they
stand still,
When we see them we get a complacent feeling
Their beauty, their simplicity satisfies our thirst
for beauty.
The enchanted scene pleases the visitors a lot
Even a coarse man, feels a feeling of pride
Because they are Legacy personified,

They are requisites for our world, for the sake of
history
How those human hands made them is a mystery
I am not talking about a person or God but a few
buildings
That are Everlasting till posterity.
They are None other but Creations that make
people wonder,
Oh yes.... They are The Seven Wonders of the
World.

– Gayatri Vyas

The Wondering Wonders

On my way to the World Heritage Sites
Going to The Great Wall of China was right.
The sun shone above the sky
It was starting of the day
It was wonderful walking on its way
Looking at the walls,
It gave me a message, "Be strong
What you do, do never wrong".

Next I went to Chichen Itza
Famous for its 'Maya' culture
A fabled city, a dynamic spectacle of old and new
The message it gave, "Incorporate the Old in New"
From Old is born the New
Change is the Law of Nature
Adapting is the best feature.

My Next Stop was Christ, the Redeemer
Standing tall amidst the burgeoning crowd
Looking at its serenity and calm
I got the message, "Be calm

Whatever comes there is no harm"
After the dark night, comes the bright Dawn

I had to see Petra
And lo behold!
It was an antiquity
What I saw was long past
Yet it gave the message
"Old Is Gold"
And never forget howsoever old.

Machu Picchu was my next Site
A city lost in the present times
Yet its Beauty beholds me
The imagination and creativity were at its peak
The message I got was, 'A thing of beauty is a joy forever'
Cherish it, Value it and it will stay forever.

I went to Italy, to see the Colosseum
Its structure impressed me the most
The amphitheatre with its vast capacity
Gave me the message "Make room for everyone"
Your love will grow stronger
No one has the power to break you
Your Love will remove the enmity
And will last a little longer.

I returned to my country India
And when I strolled into The Taj and saw around
I found myself on cloud nine

Its beauty enshrined me
I was caught in the labyrinth of Time
To see this Apostle of Eternal Love Shine
It gave me the message, "Strong is the Power of Love"
Love and be loved, that is the Spirit of Life
True Love is hard to find.

Thus ended my tour of the Wonders bright
They are the symbols of light
They are just not Wonders to be kept aside
But, are symbols of our Pride
They give the message, "Life is Beautiful"
Enjoy it, Live it and Cherish it
It will never come again
Again it can never be made
No matter how much you pay.

– Tibrata Ranjan, Vandita Sharma

"A dynamic spectacle of ancient and colourful civilization"
CHICHEN ITZA, MEXICO

My friend **Chichen Itza**, an antique 'Maya' culture land is located at Mexico. Even he accompanies me in the category of the new Seven Wonders of the World. He is the largest city of the 'Maya' culture and is very famous. Well! my friend came into this world even before me. He was born in 832 AD.

Currently, my friend is owned by the state of Yucatán. His very amazing and pretty 'Maya' name "Chichen Itza" means "At the mouth of the well of the Itza." This is derived from *chi*, meaning "mouth" or "edge," and *ch'en* or *ch'e'en*, meaning "well." In his earlier times, he participated in the water-borne circum-peninsular trade route through its port site of Isla Cerritos on the north coast, Chichen Itza was able to obtain locally unavailable resources from distant areas such as obsidian from central Mexico and gold from southern Central America. He even has one of the prettiest temple **Osario** inside his elegant and magnificent structure.

Between AD 900 and 1050 he was expanded to become a powerful regional capital controlling north and central Yucatán. Even Isla Cerritos was established as a trading port. Most of the powerful kings used him as their kingdom. He is visited by about 1.2 million people annually.

Chichen Itza is a dynamic spectacle of an ancient and colorful civilization. He was once home of thousand people but now has worn to lifeless, albeit impressive, grey stone in Maya world. He was the most diverse city in population. He is the most prominent face in the tracing of the Mayan civilization. Based on the most precise astronomical as well as astrological predictions, on the days of equinox, a special serpent feature can be seen which is cherished on the major pyramid El-Castillo.

He was a city which over flowed with the human as well as capital and mineral resources, but now has no life in it. Due to his fascinating work and art, he is the pride of the world, one of the famous seven wonders. He is the fabled city which will remain in our heart and will remain so till posterity.

It proves to be the major tourists' attraction. The pride of Mexico and symbolism of the richest ever Mayan culture, that they are not mere remains but have scope for everlasting incorporation of ancient experiences in modern developments to create the best society ever and give the mankind the most improvised ever existence. He is the most interesting wonder of the seven.

Chichen Itza

Chichen Itza well known as the "mouth of wells",
In the awesome country of Mexico it dwells.
Looking at the silent stones,
I hear thousands of different tones.

This sacred piece, such holy stone
Serendipity I see, so soft
A skill profound, brilliance of hand
Mirage to which eyes aloft.

An age craft with a blissful aura, to cherish the
poet's heart
Only to mention thou art's dimension
Crowned in the gold, a wonder there stood,
Such treat to eyes and mind.

Soul of Chichen Itza, the poet's land
Has robbed intention – So divine.
When I see the monument, I have no words.
But people are doing nothing to protect it from
hazards.

From far behind it can be identified,
That the person who made it was very dignified.
Limestone and thatch and wood above
Stood to their glory and pride.

– Ananya Pandey, Kulpreet Hora,
Shivangi Choudhary

Chichen Itza

When you go near
The first thing you will notice is
How magnificent big cities!
Larger than your hand.

When you see it,
Grasping your chest, you will utter
'Oh My God'
The reaction of uncontrollable awe.

Going up the steps
Never noticed before,
How steep, how narrow
Ninety-one steps each side,
Three hundred and sixty-five,
Three-dimensional triangular quadrant,
Projecting the art of the monolithic.

—Richa Gupta

"Like a Dragon's tail, spreading its length,
Rolling on the hills, pulsing in the Sun,
laughing at the world"

—*Timothy Bracken*

THE GREAT WALL OF CHINA

Taj Mahal: I am Taj Mahal and with me I have my dearest friend who is also one of the Seven Wonders of the World. His name is **The Great Wall of China.** He belongs to the neighbouring country China and today he will tell you about himself.

The Great Wall of China: I am a series of fortifications made of stone, brick, tamped earth, wood, and other materials, generally built along an east-to-west line across the historical northern borders of China in part to protect the Chinese Empire or its prototypical states against intrusions by various nomadic groups or military incursions by various war-like peoples or forces. My several parts were being built as early as the 7th century BC; these later joined together and made bigger and stronger and are now collectively referred to as the Great Wall which is me. Especially famous thing about me is the wall built between 220-206 BC by the first Emperor of China, Qin Shi Huang. Little of that wall remains. Since then, I am on and off been rebuilt, maintained and enhanced.

I have other purposes which include border control, allowing the imposition of duties on goods transported along the Silk Road, regulation or encouragement of trade and the control of immigration and emigration. Furthermore, the defensive characteristics were enhanced by the construction of watch towers, troop barracks, garrison stations, signaling capabilities through the means of smoke or fire, and the fact that the path also served as a transportation corridor.

'These days people may feel
they cannot make change
with mankind pitted brother against brother.
But I show them
what they can do
by just letting them put one brick on another.'

I am bigger, I am stronger, I am a place for the tourists to sight-see, and I teach people team work and unity. I am not the change but a challenge, so don't just sit idle, Get up and face it because TIME IS RUNNING....

The Great Wall of China

Chinese Slaves raised these stones
With hands, with backs, the breaking task
Leaving fractured horses, broken soldiers.

'But the wall remains, remains unbroken
Spreading its length, rolling on the hills,
Pulsing in the sun, laughing at the world.'

Built upon miles and miles of mountains,
Dotted with strong fortresses both on hilltops and ridges.
Weathering three thousand years of wind and rain
Transforms into a dancing dragon in the earth's hilly forest.

The Wall that the Emperor built
To keep their grand enterprise free
When armies had started to wilt.

– *Shivangi Chaudhary*

The Great Wall of China

Greater than you can ever imagine
Greater than you can ever see
The Great Wall of China is the one
Made with hard-work and unity.

Each brick was the hope of the worker
Because they joined together and made bigger and stronger
It was part to protect the Chinese Empire
For enemies watchful rivalry eye.

Also seen from space
Breaking the record of the longest stairs
It was built as early as 18th century
But now everyone wants it in their country.

– Vani Jha

The Optimistic Wall

The wall ever been created
The wall always has supported
Ages passed and so the centuries
To see that, people died for opportunities.

Created in last eighteen
Such a faithful wall
Stood in all aspects, cold and hot
Protecting the people in every spot.

It can even be seen from moon
Yeah its true, one who does good
Is seen by all the world
Even by all heavenly bodies.

The good deeds are always seen
And always outshine in the world
So it joins The Seven Wonders of the World.

Such a Heavy and Huge wall
Can anything be more tall.
Made in the ages of low manufacture
But is the best example of architecture.

—Bhumika Agrawal

The Great Wall of China

Standing as a series of fortification
A Sign of bravery and motivation
The sun in the space
Can see this long chain.

People made it brick by brick
So, that they could be safe from Mongols' trick
Leaving fractured horses, broken soldiers
But the wall still remains unbroken.

It is none other
But The Great Wall of China
Heavens are high and clouds are big
But they cannot be compared with it.

– Akshita Ahuja

The Great Wall of China

Not built in a day,
But with the great effort of Chinese slaves.
Qui Shi Huang was the only leader,
To fight against the enemy dreader.

The people broke, the situation broke,
But the wall remains, remains unbroken.
Then comes the turn of the wall,
Then laughs at the world, pulsing in the sun.

The wall was composed of stone, bricks and all that was available.
The emotion was one to protect its people from the enemy dreader.
Built on mountains, spread from east to west,
Even when attacked it did not break and did not get mixed with the rest.

Seen from the moon,
But not built so soon. Built on the boundary,
To protect its own country,
Its the Great Wall of China.

— Shivangi Chaudhary

"Full many a flower is born to blush unseen and waste its sweetness on the desert air."

—*Thomas Gray*

CHRIST THE REDEEMER, BRAZIL

Christ the Redeemer', a wonderful statue of Jesus Christ situated on Morro do Corcovado (Corcovado Hills) in Rio de Janeiro, Brazil, South America is one of Seven Wonders of the World. He is the statue of Redeemer meaning Jesus and is the tallest statue of Jesus Christ in the world. His whitish colour gives a beautiful impact in the blue sky. From above, the vehicles look like tiny ants moving to their destinations. Brazil looks beautiful from there. This place is declared as the holy place for Christians. There is a crowd on Christmas Eve, Good Friday and other holy festivals. He has his own importance.

He is the country's most distinguished landmark. From his mountain top, he watches over the city. His arms are stretched wide open to invite everyone from all walks of life to come and visit. In Portuguese, He is Christo Redentor. In English, He is Christ the Redeemer.

He is one of the most recognizable and popular sights in Rio de Janeiro. He is 98 feet tall and his arms are stretched about 92 feet. He stands on a square stone pedestal base which is about 26 feet high. He is considered an icon of Rio de Janeiro and Brazil. Also, he is Brazil's most famous monument.

Christ the Redeemer was completed in 1931. He weighs approximately 635 tonnes. He was named one of the new Seven Wonders of the World in 2007. French sculptor Paul Landowski beautifully carved him while the engineer Heitor da Silva Costa of Brazil built it. He has been built with reinforced concrete and soapstone. It was the first time that mosaic would be used on a statue. Da Silva Costa, whose design was chosen in February 1922, imagined the statue facing the rising sun.

A symbol of the city and a source of inspiration for countless artists, He, makes up one of the Seven Modern Wonders of the World.

Like the statue, everybody embraces – and is embraced in return.

The Statue of Inspiration

You, the statue of Jesus Christ,
The idea of Vincentian priest;
You, "The Statue of Inspiration",
Help a person overcome depression;
Oh! You are a deity.

Hands, like the wings of an angel,
As if trying to embrace our pain.
You make us forget, What we have lost,
And help us remember, What we have to gain.
Oh! You are God.

Surviving the changing mood of nature,
Even anger of nature is unable to make you denature;
Your face reflects the grace of Almighty,
Giving hope to the person - flighty;
Oh! You are a deity.

You grant us courage,
To face difficult situations and disgrace;

Standing straight, overlooking the city,
From top which seems a little bitty;
Oh! You are God.

—Soumya Mishra

The Gift of Christ

635 tonnes, 30 metre long,
Was not that easy to build
Salute those, who handed it over
To us, to the World!
Yes, it is the Redeemer
The Gift of Christ, the Gift of God.

In the heart of Brazil,
Lies this beautiful site, and also
In the heart of us, the People!
Yes, it is the Redeemer
The Gift of Christ, the Gift of God.

—Pranavi Kakani

Christ the Redeemer

Rio Di Janerio's heritage,
Standing on a very high stage
Then also a bow head
Shows the serenity ahead.

Its authentic art,
Enchants the visitors a lot
It portrays the Christian belief
A messiah, a relief,
It is a sign of liberty
May we remember him heartily.

—Sanskriti Bhardwaj

"While stands the Colosseum, Rome shall stand;
When falls the Colosseum, Rome shall fall;
And when Rome falls-Shall fall the World."

—*Lord Byron*

THE COLOSSEUM, ITALY

I am Taj. I am standing in the grounds of Agra, India. I am one of the Seven Wonders of the World. I have already told you about my friends Chichen Itza, The Great Wall of China and Christ, the Redeemer. Now let me introduce you to the **The Colosseum**, who was included among the New seven Wonders of the World, following a competition organized by New Open World Corporation (NOWC), in 2007. Built in 72 AD, the Colosseum has remained one of the largest amphitheatres in the world. He is also the most popular tourist attraction in Rome.

Words cannot describe the feeling and awe of this place. To think, he has lasted this long and still is as beautiful now as he was in the beginning. He is probably the most impressive sight in Rome. It is hard to imagine how such a massive structure was erected so long ago. It gives me the sense that we are not quite intelligent as we think we are.

The Colosseum in Rome has 80 entrances and can accommodate about 50,000 spectators. The Colosseum in Italy took only nine years and 60,000 Jewish slaves. But I, Taj, took 17 years and about 22,000 people to build.

Today, in the 21st century, he stays partially ruined because of damage caused by devastating earthquakes and stone-robbers, still, he is an iconic symbol of Imperial Rome. He is one of Rome's most popular tourist attractions and has close connections with the Roman Catholic Church, as each Good Friday the Pope leads a torchlit "Way of the Cross" procession that starts in the area around him.

The Colosseum is also depicted on the Italian version of the five-cent euro coin.

He is amazing and I, Taj am speechless about it.

The Roman Colosseum

Colosseum is a beautiful place
Beautiful very much
That everyone likes it too much.
The sun still rises in the east
And darkness falls at night.

But Colosseum is the same
Shining very bright.
When I pass near the walls
And the deep shadow falls
Imagination brings back
Those ancient Romans and war like men.

When I approach to get a closer view, all the history comes alive
When the stairs I climb, I forget the precious time
It is the place of victories won and of history unknown
Coliseum, a place of eternal memories
Is beautiful more than the fairies.

– Aditi Gaur

The Colosseum

Built with eighty entrances,
The grand Colosseum,
The Flavian amphitheater,
Situated in Rome,
The largest in the Roman Empire.

Used for games like playing with fire,
Gladiatorial contests; mock sea battles,
And re-enactments of famous battles,
Platform of classical mythology,
Stands eternal defying chronology.

Iconic symbol of Imperial Rome,
Built of everlasting concrete stones,
Way of cross procession led by the Pope,
The Good Friday parade lights up the hope.

This Flavian of ten million stones,
Recalls those ten thousand souls,
Whose cries of triumphs and thwarts,
And rejoicing in the royal sports.
Echoes in its Hall.

—Shalu Bhati

Colosseum – The Iconic symbol of Imperial Rome

At the center of the Rome city,
Constructed by the emperors of the Flavian dynasty,
Stands one of the seven wonder – the Colosseum,
The Iconic symbol of Imperial Rome.

Also known as the Flavian Amphitheater,
And considered one of the greatest works of Roman architecture,
Built of concrete and stone,
Is the Iconic symbol of Imperial Rome.

It looks very beautiful at night,
With about forty-eight meters of height,
Located just east of the Roman Forum,
The very Iconic symbol of Imperial Rome.

—Ankita Nanglia

"Beautiful art and ingenious engineering,
The ingenuity of the Nebataean people is remarkable."

PETRA, JORDAN

I again come back to my Continent of Birth – Asia. I am full of pride that my continent can yet again boast about another wonder of the world. Can you believe it, that the people of this continent, can be so good in architecture. I will now introduce you to Petra.

One of the most interesting and ancient places of world called Jordan near Egypt is famous for its statues, neighbouring country of Mummies, and also for PETRA one of the seven wonders of the world.

The Nabataeas built Petra in 500 BC. He was very vast when he was built, but a destructive earthquake destroyed his many buildings. Since 1985, he has become a UNESCO- protected monument.

Famous writers have written amazing poems on him and they also identify Petra as the capital of the Nabateans and the centre of the caravan trade.

One of the best descriptions about Petra has been given by the poet **John W. Burgon**

'A Rose Red City Half As Old As Time.'

The Petra

It is majestic
Not to be conquered
It is a wonder
That has been marked
On the sand, in the gloom
Rosy like flowers on bloom
Holy, with the hand of might
It has been made in the desert plight.

Rock Out Architecture

Across the rose-red blush we wandered,
Promising us adventures and mysteries....
Capital city of Nabateans.
Standing on slope of Jebel-Al-Madbhah,
Discovered by Johann Leudswig Burckhaardt.

Beautiful cleft in the rocks,
Featured in 'Indiana Jones',
Novels, poems and songs.
Lost city with Royal tombs,
Impressive and unimpressive both.

Men built 7,000 seat amphitheatre
Started by Nabateans,
Expanded by the Romans.
The Roman Highway standing in front,
As if man looking towards the vaults.
Sand, art, natural and real....

Rock–cut architecture dazzles at night.
Bedouins wander around, with only
Western Geldersman that ever lived.
But flood, erosion eating you now,
Oh God! Not again, Rose city lost again
By the ravages of time.

– Mamta Phogat, Morewe Mall,
Priti Sheoran, Pallavi Sharma,
Saroj Choudhary, Vartika Rai

Petra

A rose-red city, half as old as time,
Known for its beauty, antiquity and shine.

A beautiful hillside hollowed out into caves,
A spectacular fortress for the Jordan braves.

An artificial oasis in a barren desert city,
The major hotspot of trade and tranquility.

Cultural crossroad between the brimming Middle-
East,
Added by UNESCO, in the seven wonders' list.

Nabateans' capital and center of caravan trade,
The most wonderful city, man has ever made.

—*Asawari Keskar, Ishika Mohanka*

Petra

A wonderful creation of the Almighty
Petra of Jordan, also called the Rose City
Famous for its architecture classy and magnificent
And a water conduit system very efficient

It's said that before we breathe our last,
We should see this awesome place at any cost.

Just a meagre part discovered by the Archeologists,
There is much more to be brought to the light.

A truly precious cultural heritage indeed,
Rightly one of the Seven Wonders of the World.

– Poorva Kataria

Wonder

Petra an ancient city in Jordan
A wonder which challenges the Modern
God's own creation.

Destroyed by nature
Earthquake is the danger
But still remains a wonder.

The damage is so bad
People feel so sad.
Nabateans made it a treasury
Its Petra monastery.

An ancient city of Middle East
But, is still the best.
Petra, an ancient city in Jordan
Is a wonder that challenges the Modern.

— Shreya Saini

"Life is not measured by the breaths you take but by those that take your breath away."

—*Phillip James Bailey*

MACHU PICCHU, PERU

Its height touches the sky,
From air to air, as through an empty net,
And is wonder of wonders,
It's the Machu Picchu.

South America boasts of yet another wonder - Machu Pichu, Peru. Machu Picchu is an amazing and beautiful wonder of the fifteenth century. He has retained his beauty till now. He is ranked sixth amongst the wonders of the world. Many archeologists believe that Machu Picchu was constructed as a royal estate of sorts, and had been built by Pachacuti Inca Yupanqui, the ninth ruler of the Inca.

He has a number of structures that enhances his beauty. He was built in the classical Inca style, with polished dry stone walls. His three primary structures that increase its pride are the Inti Watana, the Temple of the Sun and the Room of the Three Windows. These are located in what is known by archeologists as the Sacred Districts of Machu Picchu.

Machu Picchu

The beauty of Machu Picchu,
Makes me emotional.
On seeing greenery all around.

You fulfill my dream of watching you,
You have become a part of my life
And I cannot forget you.

You are one of the wonder,
You tell everyone to live happily.

You keep everyone's soul in you forever tightly,
Machu Picchu, you are the most wonderful place,
And will remain in my heart always.

—Sakshi Saini

Stones of Machu Picchu

The ground is dry this morning
And is hard as concrete
Where the world lies
Like a stone hill.

What does one make of it,
Small stones, as small as my hand
Yet, they carry their rough silence
that tells us its entire story.

– Shreya Gupta

Machu Picchu, the Lost City

Machu Picchu, the lost city,
Stands with its authentic pride in society
Full of auspicious glory
Is ready to tell its untold story.

The different Stone Age structures
Display a scene, incredible
All gathered at one place for a panicle
With art full of grace
It is difficult to find another trace.

The historic city carved out of hill
Makes us feel, all structures
Are made with a stencil
The view is so hypnotic
Full of beauty and majesty!

—Muskan Bishnoi

Machu Picchu

Look upon my beauty
Standing with Pride.
In the land of mummies
Irregular and wide.

Surrounded by clouds and fog
Somewhere high, somewhere low.
I chill around with birds flying
Side by, the river flows.

Nature around makes me look green
As if saying to the world 'Go Green'
But time is destroying me
Standing alone for the time being.

—Aditi Vashishtha

"Let the splendor of diamond, pearl and ruby vanish? Only let this one teardrop, this Taj Mahal, Glisten spotlessly bright on the cheek of time, forever and ever."

—Rabindranath Tagore

TAJ MAHAL, INDIA

So, now I have told you all, about the other wonders, who are the pride of their makers, who dreamt about it and made their dreams come true. We, The Seven Wonders, though in different countries, can boast about our architecture and rich heritage which is being passed on from one generation to the other.

Now let me get back to my story. Let me tell you about myself….

It is a beautiful full Moon night. I can feel the dainty Moon light illuminating myself. I feel the serenity of the enchanting light. I can see the beautiful Yamuna river flowing peacefully along its way. In the still waters, I see my reflection. The clear and exquisite reflection delights me. Now I understand why the people all over the world crave for my glance. In this delightful moment, I slowly recall those long 375 years since my birth.

Somehow I still can hear in this tranquility, the Mughal emperor Shah Jahan crying like a baby at Mumtaz's tomb. Mumtaz Mahal was the beloved wife of Prince Khurram (later known as Shah Jahan), whose real name was Arjumand Bano Begum. Shah Jahan was prominently influenced by her unusual charm, sincerity and pleasing manners. She was his chief advisor and an ideal affinity, who stood by him through thick and thin. In all, they spent eighteen happy years of married life. But at the time of giving birth to one of her children, she became seriously ill. No stone was left unturned to save her but all the efforts went in vain. She ultimately died on 17 June 1631 in Burhanpur. She was just 39 years old. The whole empire was shrouded in grief on the death of this noble lady. The tears of distressed Shah Jahan that I have seen, were probably not just for grief of his separation from his wife but perhaps, of remorse for he might have held himself responsible for her death at such an early age. The reason was in due course of their short-term marriage, she had given birth to 14 children that took a toll on her and she died after delivering their fourteenth child.

In vain, to overcome his regret and grief, Shah Jahan was determined to build such an Epitaph that would immortalize Mumtaz and his love for her. He wanted her to be remembered by people all over the world till posterity and so I, the Taj Mahal, came into existence. And thus everyone regards me as the epitome of love.

My construction, is another saga of its times. 'The lady of the Taj' - Mumtaz Mahal was given a temporary burial in Burhanpur. Her dead body was sent to Agra in December 1631 A.D. and was again buried temporarily under a temporary structure on the banks of river Yamuna. Shah Jahan invited designs for Mumtaz's memorial from all over the world. He chose Ustad Isa Afandi of Turkey as the chief architect. Thus, I now reveal the name of my so-called father, who brought me into existence and gave me such an elegant look that is marveled all over the globe. Another challenging task was to select a suitable location for my construction. Shah Jahan selected a place about one and a half mile away from the Agra city on the banks of the river Yamuna. This was a perfect sight, as it was away from the chaos of the city. The U-shaped Yamuna river reduced the venture of my destruction due to flood and assured a constant supply of water. Also this location was clearly visible from Agra fort.

So, the construction began. I remember the mighty parade of about 20,000 workers, carrying armful of tools and working from morn till night, carving beautifully on my body. I clearly remember those days of mine, when I was being carved and shaped and moulded by those skilled workers. My creators were given a living space just in front of my entrance, the southern gate. The colony still exists and is known as Taj Ganj.

My construction took complete 22 years. The evidences are 22 small dome-shaped structures, eleven each on back and front sides, respectively of the main entrance.

The completion of my construction was a period of joy. I can recollect how those several workers were jubilant as they got the first glance of the complete me. How they marveled at their creation! How Shah Jahan was satisfied with his wife's epitaph, the mesmerizing mausoleum! I have seen this all. I have seen the workers dancing around jovially, contented at their achievement. But the long-driven myths claim that their joy did not last long. It is said that the hands of all these workers were brutally chopped off, so that they could not build any other Taj Mahal. But I cannot recall such sorts of things happening around me. Well, these are all myths. What actually happened was, these workers were given a lot of wealth, more than enough for feeding their complete eight generations, on the condition that they would no longer work for anybody under any circumstances. This is similar to restraining their freedom and thus, their hands were said to be chopped off.

As I continue to stare at myself in the reflection, I cannot stop myself marveling at the beautiful and intelligent architecture I am gifted with. I am not fond of blowing my own trumpet. But this full Moon night my hidden soul has awakened, that tells me what actually I am.

I have three entrances, the southern gate, the eastern gate and the western gate. All the three gates lead to my main entrance. Throughout the day, I see lakhs of tourists from all over the world approaching me through these gates. Then comes the beautiful garden. It is divided into four equal parts and in the corner lies me. Fountains and running channels of water with large reservoirs are typical of the garden design. Water was earlier drawn from Yamuna river and was stored in overhead tanks, from where it was supplied to the gardens. As one slowly approaches towards my main building made up of white marble – that becomes exquisitely radiant on full-moon nights and is eye-pleasing and mesmerizing for all my admirers – one admires my ever increasing size one notices. For one's astonishment, I am 244 feet tall – that makes me taller than Qutub Minar. I am a perfect concoction of Indian and Persian culture and my pinnacle is a perfect presentation of that. My pinnacle is about 30 feet high – about one-eighth of my total height. At the top of my pinnacle, there stands a 'Kalash' with a coconut in it, lying on two Mango leaves. It is the symbol of Hindu culture. Then comes the crescent Moon with diameter of about four feet, followed by two goglets (*surahi*), symbolic of Persian culture. Then comes the inverted lotus, whose petals are about 18 feet long, which rests on my dome. This inverted lotus is a symbol of sorrow in both Indian and Persian culture.

My astonishingly beautiful dome is actually a double dome structure – a hollow dome rested on a hollow cylinder. Then, follows the main building. In the side compartments, on the eastern side, there are masjids and in the West – Mehmankhana. At the centre lies the heart and soul of Shah Jahan – the tomb of Mumtaz Mahal. On its sides, lies the tomb of Shah Jahan himself. But what is visible are not the actual tombs, the actual tombs are hidden deep inside me in a hidden compartment underground where entry is now restricted. This is the place, where I remember the grief-stricken Shah Jahan shedding tears. My main building is cordoned by four minars on all the four corners. These 'minars' are tilted towards the outside by 5 cm, so as they do not fall on me in case of any calamity such as earthquake and lead to my demolition.

From my backyard, one can marvel at the serene and charming crescent Yamuna river. From my railings, the Jasmine tower of Agra fort is clearly visible and probably I am quite clearly visible from this place. This is the place where Shah Jahan was held prisoner by his son, Emperor Aurangazeb. I remember gazing him at me day and night from the prison and recalling those memorable days spent with Mumtaz. I have seen him taking his very last breath looking at me from the tower.

Another structure visible from the railings is the incomplete, black Taj Mahal across the river. It is commonly said that Shah Jahan intended to build a similar structure like me for his own burial, but could not complete it. But it is not true. As far as I remember, it was a kind of pleasure garden where Shah Jahan used to sit at nights and gaze at my reflections in the pond. Another interesting part is that the distance between me and my so-called cousin, the black Taj Mahal, is same as that between me and my main entrance. Thus, one can think of it as being a part of my Taj complex itself.

INDIA.........**My Country**, is home to many worth seeing historical places. Agra is just one of them. I am proud to say that, I am the only feature of Agra that reflects the Mughal heritage.

My joy knew no bounds when students of Birla Balika Vidyapeeth came to visit me. I was filled with immeasurable joy to see them.

It was a bright, sunny day and all those students were thrilled to see me. My beauty was something beyond their description. I am a dream in marble which was built by Shah Jahan in sweet memory of his beloved wife, Mumtaz.

But all of them kept my history aside and got engrossed in seeing my mathematical face. They looked around my filigree work and carvings and started searching for some geometrical shapes in me. For some time, I was transformed to the marble of shapes and figures.

At first, I was a little perplexed but later on.... How interesting it was! They were surprised to know that, at present, I am higher than Qutab Minar. They felt that the story behind the verses written on me is immense. They were shocked and surprised to know that from top to bottom the size of the letters change accordingly so as to appear the same.

Since the time people felt my presence in this world, I have been visited by people from around the world. I have been widely appreciated for my beauty. So, it shocked me to see those children looking at me in a very different way or I must say looking at me uniquely.

Those children transformed me from an embodiment of love and beauty to a figure comprising of squares, rectangles, circles and what not....

I was so fascinated by them that I could not resist myself from eavesdropping at their conversation.

Anam – Wow! Garima, What a beautiful place!

Garima – Oh Yes! No wonder, it is the best of the Seven Wonders of the World.

Anam – Did you see the floral design on the walls? Isn't it so pretty?

Garima – Its perfect! I mean just look at the fine symmetry. I wonder how the workers at that time would have done it.

Anam – Hmm, They were so talented. How hard they must have worked for 20 years.

Muskan – Hey girls! What's up?

Garima – Hello Muskan! Just admiring the beauty of The Taj Mahal!

Muskan – Forget about the beauty. Just notice those amazing geometrical shapes on this monument. Look over there at the top, the cylindrical dome and the rectangular shape depicts the unity of Hindus and Muslims.

Anam – Well, that's quite interesting. I never observed that before. Thank you Muskan!

Shivangi – See, that's a cuboid (pointing to the pedestal on which the Taj Mahal is standing).

Sakshi – Did you see the four cylindrical pillars?

Aditie – Oh! And the marble is still shining after so many years.

Pallavi – Even the garden is full of so many different shapes. That means, even the people of that time were aware about the geometrical shapes and scientific knowledge.

Morewe – Look at the inverted flower on the top of the dome! I read somewhere that the inverted flower on the top of the dome is a symbol of 'death' and 'sorrow' while the erect flowers represent happiness and joy.

Muskan – The spiral designs around the door look so attractive.

Garima – Even the path on which we are walking is decorated with the shapes of hexagons.

Anam – Garima, did you notice that all of us are just paying attention to the geometrical shapes. They have changed the whole thing into maths.

Garima – Yeah! That's true. But don't you think that is something different and unique?

Anam- What do you mean by that?

Garima – I mean that may be, we students, enjoy it through mathematical interpretation. We all want to be different. Isn't it?

Muskan – Of course! Everyone has the right to interpret things as they want. Who are we to stay anything?

Garima – Sure, everyone can admire things differently.

Anam – Absolutely right!

Muskan – We have to go back. Ma'am is waiting for us.

Morewe – Wait! Wait! Wait! Before leaving, let me tell you an interesting fact about the planning of the Taj Mahal. It is said that the place where Taj Mahal is situated, represents the seat of Allah. The fountains in the garden and the Yamuna river flowing at the back of the Taj Mahal represents the river flowing in heaven which waters the gardens.

Today, I have been standing here for 375 long years. I have seen a lot many legends appreciating my beauty, ranging from all the famous celebrities of today, to the mighty Mughal emperors. They adore me and the clear blue screen behind me, which provides me as wonderful background. I am so engrossed in dealing with the countless visitors, that I seldom get an opportunity to think about myself and my beautiful existence of three and a half centuries.

Today in this tranquil, serene and peaceful night, I got this golden chance to relish and relive those 375 years of my life. I rediscovered myself in this mystic calmness and cherish each and every moment. I feel light-hearted now and am eagerly waiting for yet another day to begin and once again amidst my admirers from all over the world.

And this will continue forever....

As Rabindranath Tagore said

"I am the tear drop on the cheek of eternity
A symbol of eternal love."

I AM TAJ....

I stand on the foothills of Agra
Making everyone remember about Mumtaj and
Shah Jahan
Named after Mumtaj
I am one of the Seven Wonders
Everyone wonders, why I am a wonder.

Hundreds and thousands of visitors come to take
a look at me
And go with praises of me
Four pillars stand around me
To protect me from every phenomena.

A dome sits on my head
Giving me a beautiful look and
At my back is river Yamuna
It makes me remember Shah Jahan's tears.

Inside me there is a grave of Mumtaj
For which I am remembered....
But, after some years, everyone will know me
As a victim of marble cancer
Because of pollution,
That puts my life in danger.

– Aditi Arya

Mumtaj's Abode

Standing alone in the moonlight
With an alive heart.
Smell of love,
Still roams as a humming bird.

It is not a monument
But, the residence of Mumtaj's beauty and spirit
Not a building....
But, the king of all, The Taj Mahal.

– Chandini Chauhan

Taj Mahal – The Story Behind

In the heart of the once Mughal capital Agra,
I stand gleaming in the light.
Born from the love and compassion of a glorious pair,
Emperor Shah Jahan made the Taj Mahal.

White marble was the king's favorite stone I presume,
For you may see
Many buildings stand tall and majestic,
Made of marble, like me.

I stand at the end of the Charbagh,
Or the four gardens as you call it.
A splendid fountain in front of me,
And trees which equal my minarets as you can see.

The four minarets that surround me are all so high,
I stand in between them with my back to the clear blue sky.
Inside my cylindrical body and the dome that is my head,

There lies so low….

Beneath the earth below,
The tomb of a lovely lady,
Who lost her life while giving birth,
To a lovely baby.

The list of seven wonders holds my name,
But to admit this for me is a great shame,
My history is not as splendid as my name and fame.

The forty thousand workers who made me,
Had their hands chopped off without mercy,
All because the emperor did not want another alike.

What good did that do, I cannot perceive,
He received curses, and as for me,
The changing world and times have been cruel.

The modern days have come,
And brought with them impurities in water and air,
My marvelous white color has diminished.

I am not as majestic as I used to be,
Though people come from all parts of the world to see me,
I feel ashamed, for I no longer show them my true beauty.

The world admires me today,
But I know, by tomorrow when my remaining
glory dies,
I shall be forgotten like the ancient cities.

But I take joy in the knowledge that,
The pages of history shall always bear my name,
THE TAJ MAHAL.

– Nikita Sharma

Taj Mahal – An Epitome of Love

Visiting one of the wonders of seven,
Makes one feel present in white heaven,
The credit goes to those magical hands,
To thousand of artisans and craftsmen.

A combination of styles which are five
He made in the memory of his beloved wife,
'He' is the owner, Shah Jahan
He owns the mausoleum, Taj Mahal in Agra.

Made up of white marble,
A symbol of peace.
The only monument
An epitome of love.
Situated in Agra
With its char minarets
An amazing monument to see.

—Radhika Agrawal

The Great Taj....

Shah Jahan made for his Love,
Who was in heaven above.

We don't know its actual story,
But still it has its own glory.

Save it, for the future generations,
So, they can understand his creations.

Take oath, to save your heritage,
So that, the future remembers the vintage.

– Gaurangi Agrawal

Taj Mahal

White-marbled structure, a precious jewel,
A song of Love of a heart that dwells.
On the banks of Yamuna, a tomb on earth,
In the moonlight, illuminating bright....

A story of Love and Loss being told,
Wonder of wonders, a beauty to behold.
A sight so beautiful, that none can curb,
Taj Mahal – the eternal message of love.

– Varistha Vishnu, Aditie Gupta, Aarushi Bansal
Shivani Soni, Rimjhim Gupta

Photo Gallery

CLASS X-B

Morewe Mall, Mamta Phogat, Saroj Choudhary, Pallavi Sharma, Priti Sheoran, Vartika Rai, Muskan Bishnoi, Subia Mahmood, Isha Nagpal, Aditi Vashishtha, Aditi Arya Priya Rani, Sanidha Singh, Gaurangi Agrawal, Garima Sharma, Anampreet Rimjhim Gupta, Varistha Vishnu, Aarushi Bansal, Aditie Gupta, Shivani Soni Akshita Jain, Monika Gulia, Akshita Ahuja, Vandana Yadav, Apoorva Singla Bhumika Agrawal, Anjali Agarwal, Banshika Goenka, Sakshi Raj, Dhanvi Choudhary.

CLASS IX-A

Shreya Saini, Somya Mishra, Kavya Goel, Aditi Gaur, Radhika Agrawal, Shruti Dash, Chandini Chauhan, Jahanvi Paliwal, Shruti Somya, Pranavi Kakani, Poorva Kataria, Nikita Sharma.

CLASS X-D

Ankita Kumawat, Hritwika Singh, Gayatri Vyas, Jasmine Kumar, Tibrata Ranjan, Ms. Vandita Sharma, Sanskriti Bhardwaj, Shriyanshi Garg, Riya Sharma, Anamika, Sanover Gupta, Shalu Bhati, Ananya Varshney, Anugya Pandey, Anjali Kiroriwal, Asawari Keskar, Sonam Verma.

Students of Class IX A, B, C, D and E, X A, B, C and D with their Teachers.

References

- *Agra and Fatehpur Guide Book*, Mittal Publications
- http://en.wikipedia.org/wiki/Chichen_Itza
- http://en.wikipedia.org/wiki/Great_Wall_of_China#History
- http://en.wikipedia.org/wiki/Great_Wall_of_China#Characteristics
- http://www.britannica.com/EBchecked/topic/1435544/Christ-the-Redeemer
- http://www.softschools.com/facts/wonders_of_the_world/christ_the_redeemer_facts/76/
- http://en.wikipedia.org/wiki/Christ_the_Redeemer_(statue)
- http://www.localnomad.com/en/blog/2013/10/01/10-interesting-facts-about-the-colosseum-in-rome/
- http://en.wikipedia.org/wiki/Colosseum
- http://en.m.wikipedia.org/wiki/Petra
- http://www.poetryinternationalweb.net/pi/site/poem/item/22593/auto/Pablo-Neruda/from-THE-HEIGHTS-OF-MACHU-PICCHU